The Last Lemon

by Alison Hawes
illustrated by Tamara Anegón

'I can't get the last lemon,' said the elephant.

'I can help you,' said the goat.

'I can get on your back.'

'I can't get the last lemon,' said the goat.

'I can help you,'
said the monkey.

'I can get on your back.'

'I can't get the last lemon,' said the monkey.

'I can help you,'
said the squirrel.

'I can get on your back.'

'I can get the last lemon!' said the squirrel.

Pink B band

The Last Lemon • Alison Hawes

Using this book

Developing reading comprehension
Elephant can't reach the last lemon, so he gets help from his friends. This humorous story builds up using three language structures repeated across several pages. This challenges the reader to follow the story meaning and notice the changes in use of vocabulary. Understanding and noticing the change between *can* and *can't* is important when using this book.

Grammar and sentence structure
- Text is well-spaced to support the development of one-to-one correspondence and return sweep onto a new line of text.
- In contexts where children are learning English as an additional language, support by rehearsing the sentence structures orally before introducing the book.

Word meaning and spelling
- Check vocabulary predictions by looking at the first letter of each animal.
- Rehearse blending easy to hear sounds into a familiar word *can get*.
- Reinforce recognition of frequently occurring words *said the I*.

Curriculum links
The idea of building a tall structure can be linked to design and technology work where children can explore making towers using a variety of construction toys and junk modelling activities.

Other Pink B texts in this series can be used to develop reading two lines of text on a page and beginning to use a greater variety of simple language structures.

Learning outcomes
Children can:
- understand that print carries meaning and is read from left to right, top to bottom
- read some high-frequency words and use phonic knowledge to work out some simple words
- show an understanding of the sequence of events.

A guided reading lesson

1. Introducing the text
Give a book to each child and read the title.

Orientation
Give a brief orientation to the text: *In this story the animals try to help each other. They try to get the lemon. The story is called 'The Last Lemon'.*

Preparation
Page 2: The elephant wants the last lemon, but he can't get it. He said 'I can't get the last lemon'. Why do you think he wants that lemon?

Page 4: So the goat can help him – can you think how he can help? Yes, that's right. The goat can get on his back.

Page 6: Can the goat get the last lemon? What do you think would help?

Let's read the story to see if the animals get the last lemon.

Strategy Check
Prepare the children for checking one to one correspondence as they read independently.

Point to each word with your finger as you read – if it doesn't match, go back to the beginning of the line and try again.